W9-BER-134

IS JENNIFER JINXING WALTER?

Walter took a step back and clutched his bowling ball.

Jennifer raised both hands and wiggled her fingers at him.

Double trouble, triple jinx,
All your balls will sink, sink, sink!

Walter's bowling ball slipped from his grip onto his foot. A sharp pain shot up his toes to his brain. "Ow-w-w-w!"

Jennifer watched him hop around on one foot. "If you're nice to me, I'll break the spell," she said.

"Go away! Just leave me alone, you jinx!"

"Don't say I didn't give you a chance, Walter *Dud.*" Jennifer waited for his reaction, but Walter had hopped over to a farther lane. He wanted to take off his bowling shoes a safe distance away.

THE NEVER SINK NINE

Pinheads, Unite!

Other Skylark Books you will enjoy
Ask your bookseller for the books you have
missed

THE NEVER SINK NINE

Pinheads, Unite!

BY GIBBS DAVIS

Illustrated by George Ulrich

A SKYLARK BOOK

NEW YORK · TORONTO · LONDON · SYDNEY · AUCKLAND

RL2, 006-009
PINHEADS, UNITE!
A Skylark Book / November 1994

Skylark Books is a registered trademark of Bantam Books,
a division of Bantam Doubleday Dell Publishing Group, Inc.
Registered in U.S. Patent and Trademark Office and elsewhere.

All rights reserved.
Text copyright © 1994 by Gibbs Davis
Cover art and interior illustrations copyright © 1994
by George Ulrich
No part of this book may be reproduced or transmitted
in any form or by any means, electronic or mechanical,
including photocopying, recording, or by any information
storage and retrieval system, without permission in
writing from the publisher.

For information address: Bantam Doubleday Dell Books
for Young Readers.

If you purchased this book without a cover you should be aware that this book is
stolen property. It was reported as "unsold and destroyed" to the publisher and
neither the author nor the publisher has received any payment for this "stripped book."

ISBN: 0-553-48132-0

Published simultaneously in the United States and Canada

Bantam Books are published by Bantam Books, a division of
Bantam Doubleday Dell Publishing Group, Inc. Its trademark, consisting of
the words "Bantam Books" and the portrayal of a rooster, is Registered
in U.S. Patent and Trademark Office and in other countries. Marca
Registrada. Bantam Books, 1540 Broadway, New York, New York 10036.

PRINTED IN THE UNITED STATES OF AMERICA

1   3   5   7   9   10   8   6   4   2

CWO

For the Milwaukee home team,
Judy and Larry Moon,
Robert Thomas, Cuyler, and Amelia

CONTENTS

THE NEVER SINK NINE

Pinheads, Unite!

CHAPTER ONE

Grandpa Walt's Surprise

Walter Dodd set down his pencil with the baseball eraser and looked around his third-grade classroom. Everyone was still working on the writing assignment.

I'm the first to finish, he realized with a smile. *I'm a slow reader, but that doesn't mean I can't be a fast writer.* He felt like a real brain.

Mrs. Howard had asked everyone to write a letter to a classmate in cursive

1

writing. Walter wished he could meet the person who'd invented cursive writing. He'd give him or her a piece of his mind. Spelling was hard enough without having to connect all the letters in one long, twisty snake.

Walter silently reread the letter he'd written to Mike Lasky. Mike was his best friend and Never Sink Nine baseball teammate. The Never Sink Nine were friends on and off the baseball field. When it wasn't baseball season, they played other sports like soccer, they helped with the Special Olympics, and together they'd even discovered a dinosaur fossil.

Dear Mike,
Want to do some thing after school? I do.
Sincerely,
Walter P. Dodd

Walter looked across the aisle. Mike's tongue was sticking out as he worked on his letter to Walter. He wished Mike would hurry up and finish so he could read it. He was bored.

Maybe it's not so great finishing first after all, he thought. *Besides, no one had even noticed.*

He looked up at Pete's Joke of the Day. Every day Pete Santos wrote a different joke on the blackboard and hid the answer somewhere on the school grounds.

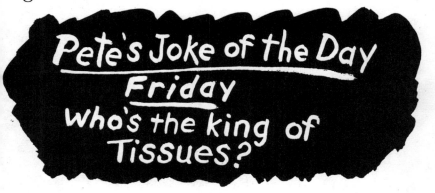

Pete's Joke of the Day
Friday
Who's the king of Tissues?

Walter gave up after a few seconds and reached inside his desk for a plastic bag filled with red clay. Whenever Mrs. Howard's students had free time, she allowed them to make things with clay. Walter spread a sheet of brown paper on his desktop and began rolling the clay into a ball. He knew exactly what he was going to make. A baseball.

In a little while, the other students had finished their letters and had taken out their clay, too. Mike was rolling a hunk of blue clay into a baseball bat and carving his name into the side with a pencil. He was the Never Sink Nine's team slugger.

Walter whispered to him from across the aisle, "Batter up."

Mike smiled when he saw Walter's baseball. After checking to make sure Mrs. Howard wasn't watching, he held up his bat and gave Walter a nod.

Just as Walter was about to pitch, Melissa Nichols turned around. She sat at the desk ahead of Walter's. A backpack bulging with toy ponies hung from her chair. "Can I have some of your clay?" she asked.

"What for? To make another pony?"

Melissa's long red ponytail swished back and forth as she shook her head. "No, I need it for my bowling ball." She held up a yellow ball of clay with three small finger holes in it. She was also a Never Sink Nine team member.

"Since when do you care about bowling?" asked Walter.

"Since my grandmother signed me up for her bowling league's tournament next week. Only grandparents and their grandkids can enter. Aren't you and Coach signed up?" Walter's grandfather was the Never Sink Nine coach.

Walter pushed his thumb deep into the clay baseball. "I don't know," he mumbled, handing over the squashed baseball. Grandpa Walt bowled in a league every Friday night. But he hadn't mentioned anything to Walter about a special tournament for grandparents and grandchildren.

"Grandpa Walt never said anything about it," Walter finally told Melissa.

"He probably just forgot to tell you." Melissa mashed Walter's red clay into her yellow ball.

Walter nodded, but he didn't really believe that. Grandpa Walt never forgot anything. In fact, he was always reminding other people about birthdays and the dates of famous baseball games.

Mike pointed to a large boy sitting a few desks in front of them. "Get a load of Otis," he whispered. Otis Hooper had made a hamburger out of green clay and was pretending to bite into it. Walter and Mike tried to muffle their laughter, but Mrs. Howard heard them.

"Since you boys have nothing better to do, would you please collect all the letters?"

"Sure," said Walter.

"Race you," Mike whispered to Walter.

Walter hurried to collect the letters on his side of the room. He was well ahead of Mike until he had to stop at Otis's desk and wait while Otis scraped a gob of clay off his letter.

Mike was already back in his seat by the time Otis finally handed over his messy letter streaked with green clay. It was a lot longer than Walter's. In fact, all the other kids' letters were longer than his. Walter decided to slip his letter on the bottom of the pile before handing them over to Mrs. Howard.

"Thank you, Walter." Mrs. Howard quickly flipped through them. "I see some very nice writing here, class." Just as Walter turned to go, she said, "Where is your letter?"

Walter shrugged. His ears burned as Mrs. Howard hunted for his letter.

"Here it is, hiding on the bottom," she said, pulling it out. "Let's take a look." A line deepened on her forehead. "This is quite short, Walter."

Walter gave a little nod. He didn't know what to say.

"A bit *too* short. Also, the margins aren't straight, there's no date, and you didn't check your spelling. I'd like you to try again over the weekend." As Mrs. Howard passed back the letter, two girls in the front row snickered. Mrs. Howard shot a stern glance at them and added, "However, your Walter P. Dodd signature is very impressive."

"Thanks." Walter sneered at the girls as he walked back to his desk. Only Mrs. Howard could tell you to do an assignment over and make you feel great at the same time.

"Beat you," Mike said as Walter took his seat beside him.

"You get the side with Otis next

time," said Walter. He looked at his Babe Ruth wristwatch. It was two forty-five. Only fifteen minutes left before class ended and the weekend began. "Want to go to Dinosaur Park after school?" he asked Mike.

That was the new name for the park where the Never Sink Nine had discovered the dinosaur fossil.

"I have piano lessons on Friday." Mike tapped his fingertips on the edge of his desk, pretending to play a keyboard.

"Oh, yeah, I forgot." Walter's plans for the afternoon disappeared.

Mrs. Howard stood at the front of the room, holding up two fingers in a **V** shape for silence. Everyone looked up and stopped talking. "Anyone with books to return to the library may go now before school is out. The rest of you will read quietly until the bell rings."

Walter didn't have to think long

before deciding what to do. He lifted his desktop and searched for a book to return. Reading books was harder than returning them. He was in a special class for slow readers.

Walter spotted a book on cowboys he had taken out of the library two weeks before. He had only gotten halfway through the first chapter. He pulled out the bookmark so no one would know. Then he put on his Never Sink Nine cap backward and slung his backpack over a shoulder to leave. "Later, alligator," he said to Mike.

Mike looked up from the book he was reading. "In a while, reptile."

Walter said good-bye to Mrs. Howard and headed out the door with Melissa and other classmates carrying books.

Inside the school library, a line of students had formed in front of Mrs. Bumby's desk, waiting to return books.

Melissa's backpack of toy horses made a rattling sound as she walked up to Walter. She held out a book. "You should read this before the bowling tournament."

Walter read the title, *Bowling for Beginners.* It was a book full of pictures, just the kind he liked. "Thanks," he said, taking it. "Want mine? It's got horses in it."

Melissa looked at the picture on the cover of cowboys on horseback. "Where are the cowgirls?"

"There aren't any."

"No, thanks," said Melissa, and took her place in line behind him.

Walter was busy reading about bowling when it was his turn.

"It's nice to see you so absorbed in a book, Walter," said Mrs. Bumby. "What's it about? Baseball, again?"

"Bowling." Walter held out the book for Mrs. Bumby to stamp and date.

"I see you're getting ready for the bowling tournament. Your grandfather said he was signing up his grandson."

"He did?" Walter could feel the grin spreading across his face.

Mrs. Bumby covered her mouth. "I hope I didn't ruin his surprise."

"That's okay," said Walter. "I won't tell." *No wonder Grandpa Walt didn't say anything,* he realized. *He's going to surprise me at dinner tonight.* Grandpa Walt ate dinner at the Dodds' every Friday night.

"My granddaughter Jennifer is visiting from out of town. We're signing up after school today."

"*You* bowl?" Even though Walter knew Mrs. Bumby was a soccer coach, it was hard imagining her anywhere but behind a library desk.

"Certainly. I'm in the Rockville Bowling League. That's where I met your lovely grandfather."

Grandpa Walt *lovely*? Walter saw Mrs. Bumby's eyes crinkle behind her glasses as she smiled. He wasn't sure, but her face looked as if it were turning pink. She handed back his book.

"I think your grandfather's going to be at Echo Bowl this afternoon," Mrs. Bumby said. "You should drop by."

"Maybe." Walter stuffed the book into his backpack and turned to go.

Melissa moved up in line to take his place. "Wait for me at the bike rack," she whispered as Walter walked past.

"Okay." Walter had nothing better to do. Mike had piano lessons, and since it wasn't baseball season, there were no Friday afternoon games. He stepped into the empty hallway and checked his watch. Five minutes left before school was out. Walter couldn't wait. He wanted to be the first student out of Eleanor Roosevelt Elementary.

He headed for the big front doors and pushed them open.

Walter jumped off the last step onto the empty yard. "I'm first!" he shouted. Once again no one was around to notice. Walter sighed and started for the bike rack. He squinted at something flapping in the breeze. It was a piece of paper taped to the steel bar.

Walter jogged over and took a closer look. It was the answer to Pete's Joke of the Day! He recited Pete's joke as he tore it off. "Who's the King of Tissues?" Then he opened the flap and read the answer.

The Hanki-Chief

Walter chuckled. "Good one, Pete."
Things were shaping up this afternoon.
He had found the answer to Pete's joke,
and he had discovered Grandpa Walt's
surprise. Just then the school bell rang.
Melissa cantered out the front door with
a stream of children. The weekend had
officially begun.

Walter waved the answer to Pete's
joke in the air. "I found it!" he shouted.
A cluster of kids, including his Never
Sink Nine teammates, gathered around
Walter as he read the answer out loud.
Pete laughed just as loud as his friends
at his own joke. Then they all said good-
bye and got on their bikes.

"I'm going to surprise Grandpa
Walt," said Walter, heading for downtown Rockville.

Melissa pulled up beside him on
her bike. "Where are you going?"

"Echo Bowl. I just remembered

some business I have to take care of," said Walter.

"What kind of business?"

"Grandpa Walt business. See you later." Walter peeled off from Melissa and waved back to her. "Boy, is he going to be surprised when he sees me at Echo Bowl!"

CHAPTER TWO

Tournament Teammates

"Hi, Dad!" Walter bicycled past his father's used-car lot in downtown Rockville on his way to Echo Bowl.

Mr. Dodd looked up from his customer and waved. "See you at dinner, son!"

Walter pedaled up Main Street past Swenson's sporting goods store. He slowed down to check the window display. No bowling balls. Two blocks later, he coasted into Echo Bowl's crowded parking lot. It was the only bowling center in Rockville, and it was always packed.

Walter left his bike leaning against the building. He had to pull hard to open the heavy front door. Walter felt as if he were stepping into a dark movie theater in the middle of the afternoon. He stood still while his eyes adjusted to the dim light. The thunderous sound of bowling balls rolling down lanes and pins crashing filled the huge open room.

Walter walked behind a dozen lanes, searching for Grandpa Walt. Along the back wall, a young man stood behind a counter covered with bowling shoes. Walter remembered the scuffed shoes he had rented the one time he went bowling with his family. He walked up to the shoe rental counter.

The man glanced down at Walter's feet. "What size? Four? Four and a half?"

He wore a bowling shirt with "SID" sewn on the pocket.

"No shoes," said Walter. "I need to know about the bowling tournament for grandkids."

"Got a grandparent in the league?"

"Walter Dodd." Walter was proud to share the same name with his grandfather.

"Your granddad's quite an athlete for an old guy." Sid handed Walter a sheet of tournament regulations.

Walter grabbed the sheet without saying thank you. Who did Sid think he was, calling Grandpa Walt an old guy? He made it sound like something bad.

Walter got himself an orange soda from the drink machine and sat down behind Lane One to read the rules sheet.

Rockville Grand Tournament

1. To be eligible, each team must consist of one grandparent and one grandchild.

2. Each grandparent must be a member of the Rockville Bowling League.
3. Each grandchild must be eight years of age or older to qualify.

"Yes!" Walter made a victory fist and pulled it down. He was eight and three-quarters. He remembered when he hadn't been allowed to play on his older brother Danny's baseball team because he was too young. That was when Grandpa Walt suggested he form his own team with kids his own age and the Never Sink Nine began.

Walter sipped his soda and watched the bowlers. They were all different ages, sizes, and shapes. It wasn't like most other sports. There were fat and thin bowlers, tall and short, young and old bowlers.

"This place is cool." Walter looked

around the dark cavelike room. Music played over the loudspeakers while people talked and bowled. He could see why Grandpa Walt liked it here. Bowling looked like fun. And when you were tired of playing, you could get food in a back room called The Grill.

Just then Mrs. Bumby walked in the front door with a girl wearing two long, skinny braids. "Walter!" The librarian waved and started toward him. "I see you beat us here on your trusty bicycle."

Walter stood up so suddenly he nearly knocked over his chair. "Hi," he said, choking on his soda. It always felt funny running into a teacher outside school.

Mrs. Bumby pushed the pale-faced girl forward. "This is my granddaughter, Jennifer Pittman."

Jennifer narrowed her eyes at Walter. "We're signing up for the tournament. I'm an excellent bowler."

Walter didn't know what to say.

"Has your grandfather signed you up yet?" asked Mrs. Bumby.

"I don't know," said Walter.

"Then why don't you look on the sign-up sheet, dummy?" Jennifer said under her breath.

Walter frowned and looked to see if Mrs. Bumby had heard what Jennifer said. She hadn't. She was standing by a bulletin board.

"Here's the sign-up sheet," said Mrs. Bumby. "Come take a look."

Walter followed behind Jennifer, feeling like a dog on a leash. All he wanted was to find Grandpa Walt.

"I'll sign us up, Grandma." Jennifer flipped her snakelike braids over her shoulders and picked up the pencil dangling from a string. She wrote in small, neat script, "Jennifer Pittman" and "Mrs. June Bumby."

Walter stood on his tiptoes, trying to see over Jennifer's shoulder.

She gave him a little shove. "Do you mind? I'm not finished."

Walter wanted to push her back, but Mrs. Bumby was standing right there. He looked around for Grandpa Walt. He couldn't wait to see their names on the sign-up sheet together. Side by side, Walter and Walter, a team. Just the thought of being Grandpa Walt's teammate made him feel special.

When Jennifer was finally done, Walter stepped up to the bulletin board and read the list of names. He found Melissa and her grandmother; Pete Santos and his grandfather; Mrs. Miller, the school crossing guard, and her granddaughter; and Mrs. Mirelli from the Pizza Palace and her grandson.

ROCKVILLE GRAND TOURNAMENT

GRANDPARENT	GRANDCHILD
Mrs. Muriel Nichols	Melissa Nichols
Roberto Santos	Pete Santos
Joan Miller	Kim Miller
Mrs. Ann Mirelli	Frankie Mirelli
Mrs. Carolyn Diaz	Joe Montoya
Edgar Hunt	Lizzy Hunt
James De La Haye	Buster Matthews
Mrs. June Bumby	Jennifer Pittman
Walter Dodd, Sr.	Danny Dodd

never realized so many people he knew liked to bowl. Finally he spotted Grandpa Walt's name. He put his finger under "Walter Dodd, Sr." and moved it across to where his own name would be.

Walter's hand dropped to his side. "Danny?" He could hardly get the name out.

"What's wrong with him?" Jennifer asked.

"Danny is Walter's older brother," Mrs. Bumby explained in a hushed voice.

"I didn't think he looked old enough to bowl in a tournament," Jennifer said.

Something inside Walter burst wide open. He spun around and faced Jennifer. "I am too, old enough! I'm almost nine, snake braids!" he yelled into her startled face.

Jennifer took a step back, but her eyes narrowed as she answered him.

"You'll be sorry. I'm going to put a jinx on you, Walter Dodd."

Mrs. Bumby stepped between them. "That's enough, children."

Walter was too upset to care.

Just then Sid yelled out from the shoe counter. "Hey, kid! Isn't that your grandfather?" He pointed toward the door. Grandpa Walt had just walked in and was talking to some friends.

Walter felt Mrs. Bumby place a hand on his shoulder. "Why don't you go over and talk to him?" she said. "Give your grandfather a chance. I'm sure he can explain."

Half of Walter wanted to run over to Grandpa Walt and demand to know why he had chosen Danny instead of him. But the other half was too hurt to face his grandfather.

Walter stood frozen to the ground, his hands clenched in fists. *He doesn't love me,* thought Walter. *He loves Danny more.* He stared at his grandfather until tears filled his eyes.

Jennifer whispered to Mrs. Bumby, "I think he's going to cry."

"Sh-h-h-h," said Mrs. Bumby.

But Walter didn't hear her. He had already bolted for the door.

Grandpa Walt saw the back of Walter's Never Sink Nine team cap as he raced past him. "Walter, is that you?" He strained to see around his friends.

Walter didn't answer or look back. He threw his weight against the heavy door and burst outside into the harsh sunlight. "What do you care?" he said, jumping on his bike. He pushed off and headed for home.

CHAPTER THREE

Walter to Walter

Mrs. Dodd called up the stairs for the third time. "Walter, your dinner's getting cold! I'm not going to tell you to come down one more time!"

Walter knew she meant it. He lifted his head from his pillow and looked outside. It was dark. He had been moping around his room since he got home from Echo Bowl. He swung his legs over the side of the bed and thought about Grandpa Walt waiting downstairs at the dinner table.

"Why should I go down?" he grumbled. "Grandpa Walt's probably just talking to Danny about their stupid tournament."

Walter heard footsteps coming up the stairs. The bedroom door opened. It was Danny.

"Mom sent me to get you."

"I'm not hungry," said Walter, looking away. Just the sight of his brother made him mad.

"Are you sick or something? You've been acting weird today." Danny picked up a baseball on his dresser. "Catch," he said, tossing it to Walter.

Walter knew Danny was trying to make him feel better. But Walter couldn't help it. He didn't even try to catch the ball. It dropped to the floor in front of him. "Leave me alone," he said, and stormed past Danny out of their room.

Downstairs Walter took his place at
the table next to Grandpa Walt without
saying a word.

"Hi there, slugger," said Grandpa
Walt. "Was that you looking for me at
the bowling alley today?"

Walter shook his head and took
a big bite of mashed potatoes so he
wouldn't have to answer. They were
stone cold.

"Funny, I could have sworn it was
you. I saw—"

Danny interrupted. "Grandpa, what
are you going to do about the tournament now that I can't be your partner?"

Walter held his breath and stopped
chewing. He didn't want to miss a word.

Grandpa Walt leaned back in his
chair. "I don't know, Danny. I forgot
all about your new paper route duties.
I guess I'll just have to drop out."

That was it! Walter was so mad he

couldn't even swallow his food. "What about me!" he shouted with a mouthful of mashed potatoes. "Don't I count?"

Everyone at the table stopped eating and stared at Walter.

Danny started to snicker. "So that's why he was acting so weird. Turkey brain." He flipped a bean across the table.

Walter ducked. "Shut up, Danny."

"That's enough, boys," said Mrs. Dodd.

Danny held both hands over his mouth as his body shook with laughter.

Grandpa Walt leaned forward and touched Walter's arm. "I never knew you wanted to bowl, sport. You never showed any interest before."

"That doesn't mean I can't be interested now." Walter wished he could get rid of the hurt sound in his voice, but he couldn't.

"You're right. It doesn't." Grandpa Walt was quiet for a moment. "Would you like to be my bowling partner for the tournament?"

Everyone at the table was quiet, even Danny. They all watched Walter, waiting for his answer.

Walter crossed his arms tightly across his chest. He wasn't going to give in so easily. "You only want me because Danny's too busy. I'm just leftovers."

"Walter, that's not fair," said Mrs. Dodd.

Grandpa Walt held up a hand. "It's okay. Walter's got a right to his opinion." He reached in his pocket for his car keys and twirled them around a finger. "What do you say we get some ice cream and discuss this, Walter to Walter?"

"Can I come?" asked Danny.

"Not this time," said Grandpa Walt. "This is between Walter and me."

Walter tried hard not to smile. He loved having Grandpa Walt all to himself.

Right after dinner, Grandpa Walt drove them across town to the best ice-cream shop in Rockville, and they both got double dips. Grandpa Walt didn't say a word as they ate their ice cream in the car. Walter knew Grandpa Walt was waiting for him to say what was on his mind. After a few minutes, Walter was ready to ask the question that had been bothering him all afternoon.

"Do you like Danny better than me?" Walter turned his face away, afraid of the answer.

Grandpa Walt gently turned Walter's face back in his direction. "No," he said, looking straight into his eyes. "I don't. You know you're my best buddy."

Walter couldn't hold back any longer. He smiled so wide his face ached. It was hard being mad at Grandpa Walt for long. "Okay," he said, taking a lick of Rocky Road ice cream. "I'll be your partner."

"Terrific. We'll make a great team." Grandpa Walt hit the horn a couple of times until the family in the car next to them turned to stare. "Look out, Rockville Bowling League! Here come the Dodds!"

"Here we come!" Walter joined in. Then he remembered a terrible thing and slumped back in his seat. "But I don't know how to bowl," he said softly.

Grandpa Walt swatted at the air. "Don't worry about that. I'm the best coach there is. All you need is a little private training. What do you say we get started right now?"

Walter nodded so hard his ice cream almost toppled off his cone.

Grandpa Walt started up the engine. "We'll stop by your house and ask your mom if you can sleep over at my place. We'll have our first official bowling lesson tonight."

Walter snapped on his seat belt and took a big bite of Rocky Road. He was going to be Grandpa Walt's teammate *and* get to sleep over at his apartment, too. For a day that had started out pretty rotten, things were shaping up.

Walter ran ahead of Grandpa Walt up the stairs to his apartment. He waited by the door, breathing in the delicious smells of chicken chow mein and sesame noodles. Grandpa Walt's apartment was right over Chung's Chinese Restaurant in downtown Rockville. Christy Chung was one of Walter's Never Sink Nine teammates.

Grandpa Walt handed the keys over to Walter. "You do the honors."

Walter immediately knew which key fit, since Grandpa Walt always let him open the door.

"Home sweet home," said Grandpa Walt, stepping into the apartment behind him.

Walter went straight to the mantelpiece to give the steering wheel mounted above it a spin. It was the steering wheel from one of the city buses Grandpa Walt had driven for twenty-eight years before retiring.

"No time for driving tonight," said Grandpa Walt, hanging up his coat. "We've got work to do. I've got a miniature bowling set in the back closet. Let's start with that."

Walter beat his grandfather to the closet and opened the door before he could be stopped.

"Watch out!" cried Grandpa Walt. An avalanche of hats, mittens, and scarves came tumbling down on Walter's head. Grandpa Walt picked up a wool hat and pulled it down over Walter's eyes. "That ought to distract the competition. You look as if you've got a bowling pin on your head."

Walter raced into the bathroom to see for himself in the mirror. The white wool hat had the same red stripe and shape of a bowling pin. It stuck straight up from his head. "I'm a pinhead," he said, making a face into the mirror. "A pinhead monster."

"Let's roll 'em!" shouted Grandpa Walt from the living room.

By the time Walter joined him, the furniture had been cleared away and the rug had been rolled back to make a mini-bowling alley. Two long pieces of rope marked the sides of the alley, and ten small plastic bowling pins stood in a diamond formation at one end near the fireplace.

Grandpa Walt laid down a yardstick

at the other end. "This will be our foul line," he said. "Try not to step over it." He handed Walter a small plastic bowling ball and helped him place his thumb and second and third fingers correctly in the holes. "Give it a try."

Walter lifted the ball high over his head and threw it through the air toward the pins. It knocked over a picture frame on a table across the room.

"Remember, this isn't baseball," said Grandpa Walt. "Keep it on the ground. Control is more important than speed."

Walter tried again. This time he placed the ball between his legs and gave it a little push. The ball crept forward and stopped short of the pins.

"Much better," said Grandpa Walt. "With a little more oomph that could have been a strike."

Eager to try again, Walter quickly retrieved the ball. "I'm just warming up," he said, certain he could knock down all the pins next time.

After a few more tries, Grandpa Walt showed him how to make his approach to the foul line and release the ball with one hand. He told Walter that a game is made up of ten frames and a bowler gets two chances to deliver the ball in each frame, unless he rolled a strike. But that wasn't likely for a beginner. Then Grandpa Walt sat in his big stuffed chair and watched Walter while he gave him pointers.

After half an hour, Grandpa Walt picked up one of the long ropes marking their private bowling alley. "That's enough for now. Tomorrow we'll practice with a real ball on a real lane. It's time to hit the sack, sport. You know the routine."

Walter loved sleeping over at Grandpa Walt's. He knew just what to do. First he helped Grandpa Walt turn out all the lights in the apartment and check the door lock. Then they went into the bathroom to brush their teeth together. Walter found his red toothbrush in its own special WALTER II cup in the medicine cabinet. He sat on the edge of the sink while they hummed "Take Me Out to the Ball Game" until it was time to rinse and spit. It was their official toothbrushing song.

Grandpa Walt always gave him the top to one of his pajama sets to wear. This one was covered with bears and tiny trees. It fit perfectly once Walter pushed up the sleeves.

Walter took a running dive onto Grandpa Walt's enormous bed. He knew just which side was his and how many pillows he was allowed to have. He snuggled under the covers and watched Grandpa Walt empty all the coins from his pockets into a big baseball trophy on his dresser. As a younger man he had played in the minors for a baseball team called the North Dakota Nine.

Next came the part Walter loved best. Grandpa Walt liked to read before turning out the lights, and he always had books from the library for Walter to read, too. Walter had noticed that when he was tired, Grandpa Walt sometimes offered to read out loud to him.

Walter yawned loudly and rubbed his eyes. "Boy, I'm a wreck," he said, repeating something he had heard his father say at the end of an especially hard day.

Grandpa Walt lowered his glasses and looked at him. "Want me to read to you tonight?"

"Okay." Walter smiled as he handed his book over to Grandpa Walt and leaned his head on his shoulder.

After a few pages, Grandpa Walt closed the book and took off his glasses.

"What should I dream about?" Walter asked. He knew Grandpa Walt wouldn't laugh.

"How about dreaming up a name for our team?"

Walter looked at the bowling pin hat he'd hung on the bedpost. "The Pinheads," he said, watching Grandpa Walt's reaction.

Grandpa Walt laughed. "I like it. I hereby officially declare us the Pinheads." He turned out the light.

"The Pinheads," Walter whispered in the dark. It sounded right.

"Night, sport."

"Night." Walter closed his eyes and drifted back through his day. School, dinner, the bowling alley, Mrs. Bumby, the sign-up sheet, Jennifer, the jinx. Walter's eyes popped open as he remembered Jennifer's words: *You'll be sorry. I'm going to put a jinx on you, Walter Dodd.*

Walter reached over and tugged on Grandpa Walt's shoulder. "What happens when someone puts a jinx on you?"

"It's supposed to bring bad luck. Why? Did someone put a jinx on you?"

"Mrs. Bumby's granddaughter."

"Don't worry," said Grandpa Walt, turning over on his side. "She just wants to scare you. It's a lot of hocus-pocus nonsense."

Walter relaxed a little. If Grandpa Walt said it was nonsense, it was nonsense. Still, he couldn't forget the look on Jennifer's face when she said it.

CHAPTER FOUR

The Jennifer Jinx

Saturday morning after breakfast the Pinheads drove to Echo Bowl to continue training for the Grand Tournament.

"You'll need some bowling shoes." Grandpa Walt headed for the shoe rental counter. He didn't need any for himself. He owned his own pair of bowling shoes.

"Meet you there in a second." Walter had something important to take care of first. He jogged over to the bulletin board and erased Danny's name on the sign-up sheet. Then he carefully printed his own name in big capital letters. Just as he was finishing, someone walked up behind him and spoke.

"Only babies print."

Walter spun around ready to fight. He found himself face-to-face with Jennifer. She was deliberately blocking his way.

"Don't you know cursive yet?"

Walter wanted to answer, but Jennifer's stare held him like glue. "Move," he said weakly.

"You better be nice to me or I'll double jinx you."

She pointed her index finger at him and began making small circles in the air as she chanted her curse.

Dribble, drabble, gurble, gop,
Your bad luck will never stop.

All your balls go in the gutter,
Plunk! One right after the other!

As her finger zeroed in and landed on his nose, Walter went cross-eyed. He shook his head to break the spell. "Move," he said more firmly, and broke away. He jogged over to the safety of the shoe counter and hid behind Grandpa Walt. He peeked out from under Grandpa Walt's arm. "She *double* jinxed me this time."

Jennifer raised both hands and wiggled all her fingers at him.

Walter ducked behind Grandpa Walt. "Look! She's doing it again!"

Grandpa Walt glanced in Jennifer's direction. "Don't be silly, Walt. She's just putting on her bowling shoes. You better start doing the same thing or we'll be stuck on Lane Twelve."

Walter looked again. This time Jennifer was tying on her shoe. She

waved at them as if nothing had happened.

"Hi, Mr. Dodd," she said sweetly. "Hi, Walter."

Walter couldn't believe it. It was as if Jennifer had turned into another girl.

"Hello, Jen." Grandpa Walt waved back. "Tell me, where's that beautiful grandmother of yours?"

Mrs. Bumby, *beautiful*? Walter stared at Grandpa Walt as if he'd gone crazy.

"She's in the ladies' room changing her clothes," said Jennifer. "Want me to get her?"

"No, don't bother. I'll be seeing her later tonight anyway," said Grandpa Walt. "We have a dinner date."

Walter's jaw dropped open. "You can't date her! She's my librarian."

Grandpa Walt chuckled and reached over to tousle his hair. "Too late. We've been going out for a month now. Besides, she's not school property, you know." Grandpa Walt handed Walter his bowling shoes. "We met at the Y, swimming."

"She *swims?*" Walter couldn't imagine Mrs. Bumby bowling, much less doing the backstroke. Librarians were supposed to stay in libraries.

"Fifty laps a day," said Grandpa Walt with pride. "Quite a woman. She lives alone like me. It's nice having someone to eat dinner with."

Walter silently followed his grandfather to their lane and put on his bowling shoes. Grandpa Walt ate dinner at his family's house every Friday night. But Walter had never thought about whom Grandpa Walt ate with the other nights of the week or what it might be like for him living alone.

Pete Santos and his grandfather were on the lane next to theirs. Pete had just finished bowling a frame and was jumping up and down.

"I made a spare!" he shouted.

"Great." Walter couldn't remember what a spare was, but he didn't want to look stupid.

Pete strutted across to their lane. "My granddad and I are calling ourselves *Trueno.* That means 'thunder' in Spanish. What's your team name?"

"The Pinheads," said Walter. Next to Thunder, it sounded babyish.

Pete made a face and laughed. "The Pinheads. That's funny. I like it." He pointed across the alley to Melissa Nichols and her grandmother. "They're the Pony Express."

"Figures." One of Melissa's toy horses was standing on their score table. Walter looked around for signs of Jennifer. He was about to tell Pete about the jinx when Grandpa Walt dumped a bowling ball into his arms.

"Time for us Pinheads to roll."

Walter carried the big plastic ball to the front of their bowling lane and dumped it at his feet.

"Ready to give it a try, sport?"

"I don't know how."

"Yes, you do. Pretend you're back in my apartment on our private bowling alley. Just zero in on the center of the lane, and go for it."

Walter had a feeling this wasn't going to be as easy as last night. Grandpa Walt helped him position his fingers in the ball.

"Okay, now zero in on the headpin," said Grandpa Walt.

Walter looked at the center pin at the far end of the lane. It could have been ten miles away instead of just sixty feet. He knew he'd have to throw hard if the ball were going to make it all the way down to the pins. He swung the ball back, took a couple of steps, and threw it forward with all his might. The ball clunked down hard on the wood boards and rolled straight toward the pins.

"Fantastic!" Grandpa Walt sounded excited.

Walter couldn't believe his eyes. The ball plowed through the pins with a loud clatter. The rack picked up the remaining pins before the sweeper bar lowered and swept away all the fallen pins. Only two were left standing.

Grandpa Walt gave him a pat on the back. "Terrific, Walt. That's an eight count. You knocked down eight pins." He shouted over to Pete's grandfather on the next lane. "José! Look at this! My grandson practically rolled a strike his first time out!"

Walter couldn't stop smiling. Bowling was fun.

"If you knock down the rest of the pins, it's called a spare," explained Grandpa Walt.

Walter nodded, but he didn't really understand how to score. All he knew for sure was he wanted to knock down all the pins just like Pete. He grabbed the ball as it popped up from the ball return and swung it back and forth a couple of times. "I'm warming up," he said.

"Sure," said Grandpa Walt. "Every bowler's got his own style. Look at Mr. Santos."

Pete's tall grandfather held the bowling ball in front of his eyes and peered over it. Walter thought he looked like an old-fashioned photographer leaning over a camera on a tripod.

"When's he going to roll it?" asked Walter.

"Watch. He's taking aim on the pins."

Mr. Santos made tiny adjustments to the right and left, up and down, before finally rolling the ball. He slowly approached the foul line and delivered the ball in one long, controlled movement.

"Smooth." Grandpa Walt nodded approvingly.

"Too slow," said Walter. "Watch me." He held the ball up in front of his face, pretending to take aim like Mr. Santos. Then he did a skip step to the foul line, bent one knee, and released the ball. Walter watched helplessly as the black ball curved widely to the left, toward the gutter. At the last second it swerved back and skimmed the side of a pin, knocking it over and bringing down the remaining pin with it.

"I did it!" shouted Walter. He turned to see who else had seen. Melissa waved from a far lane.

Grandpa Walt gave him a pat on the back. "You did it, sport. Your first spare."

Mr. Santos had seen, too. "You're a natural, Walt. Just like your *abuelo*."

Walter knew *abuelo* meant "grandfather" in Spanish.

Grandpa Walt couldn't hide his smile as he unzipped his bowling bag and pulled out his magnificent dark green ball with black swirls. It was his personal bowling ball. Only the veteran players had their own balls.

"Can I hold it?" asked Walter.

"It's heavy," warned Grandpa Walt, handing it over.

Walter cradled the monster ball in his arms. "Wow. It weighs a ton."

"Sixteen pounds."

"That's eight pounds more than mine." Walter ran a hand over its smooth surface.

Sid from the shoe rental counter sat overlooking Walt's lane while taking his break. "You're a sure thing for first place, kid. Anyone lucky enough to bowl with the Kingpin is bound to win the trophy."

"The Kingpin?"

"That's your granddad's nickname around here. Didn't you know that? He's the strongest senior player in the league."

Walter shook his head. He was beginning to realize there was a lot he didn't know about his grandfather.

Nearly everyone paused to watch as Grandpa Walt approached his lane. He took aim by focusing on the arrows on the alley. Then he released his green and black ball with a powerful arm swing. The ball spun across the wooden boards as if on ice and collided dead center into the pins with a thunderous crash.

Several people clapped. *Grandpa Walt's a celebrity,* Walter thought. *And I'm his grandson. That makes me a celebrity, too.* Walter never thought he'd feel this way, but bowling with Grandpa Walt was almost better than playing baseball. On the baseball field Grandpa Walt was the Never Sink Nine coach, but here at Echo Bowl, they were teammates.

Walter and Grandpa Walt continued to bowl for more than an hour. It seemed as if everyone signed up for the tournament was there practicing, too.

When it was time for a lunch break, Walter and his grandfather headed for The Grill in the back room. Walter loaded his tray with a grilled cheese sandwich, potato chips, an orange, and a carton of chocolate milk.

"Hey, Walter! Over here!" Pete waved from a table with Melissa, Mike, and Tony. Mike and Tony had dropped by to have lunch with them.

"Go on and sit with your friends," said Grandpa Walt before Walter had a chance to ask. "I'm going to join Mrs. Bumby and some of the other grandparents."

"Okay." Walter loved being with Grandpa Walt, but he was glad to see his friends. There were some things only another kid could understand. The Never Sink Nine were always cheering one another on. He carried his tray over to the table and sat down.

"I saw you bowling with Coach," said Mike. "He's awesome. You're lucky your grandfather lives in Rockville instead of Montana like mine."

"Yeah," added Tony sadly.

Walter knew Tony Pappas's grandfathers were both dead. It made him feel grateful to have Grandpa Walt. He looked over at Grandpa Walt's table. He was sitting with Mrs. Bumby, Mrs. Nichols, Mr. Santos, and Jennifer. Walter quickly looked away, in case Jennifer tried to jinx him again.

"Think we should ask Jennifer to sit with us?" asked Melissa. "I don't think she knows anybody here."

Walter nearly choked on a potato chip. "No way," he said, coughing. "She tried to jinx me."

Melissa stopped trotting her toy pony across the table and leaned forward. "Jinx you? What do you mean?"

Tony got out his pencil and notepad, ready to take notes. He was always looking for a good story for his newsletter for kids, the *Rockville Rookie Report.*

Walter tried to describe it. "She does this weird thing with her fingers, and then she puts a spell on me."

"What kind of spell?" Tony was jotting down everything.

"A spell to roll gutter balls."

"Did it work?" asked Mike.

"Nah." Walter forced a laugh. "That's just a lot of hocus-pocus. I threw one gutter ball all morning."

"It sounds like witchcraft," whispered Melissa. Everyone at the table turned to look at Jennifer.

"Only time will tell." Tony flipped his notepad shut and got up to leave. "I promised to help Dad at the store this afternoon. We got in a new shipment of faucets and plungers." Mr. Pappas owned the Never Sink Plumbing Company, the Never Sink Nine's team sponsor.

"I'm going to help, too," said Mike, putting on his jacket.

After lunch, everyone went back to bowl a line. As the afternoon wore on, the crowd thinned out. Walter looked around at some of the empty lanes. Pete and Melissa had already gone home with their grandparents.

Grandpa Walt began peeling off the wrist supporter he wore on his bowling arm. "We've put in a good day's practice, sport. What do you say we go home after you play this frame?"

"Okay." Walter knew if he got a spare or a strike in the tenth frame,

63

he'd get bonus balls. Even though he didn't know his score yet, it felt good knowing he had steadily improved all day. Walter gripped the ball in the three finger holes and approached the lane. He heard Grandpa Walt's voice behind him. "Remember, zero in." Then he heard another voice.

"Break a leg."

Walter's arm turned to jelly. His bowling ball sank to his side as he turned around and saw Jennifer sitting on the railing behind their lane.

"Good luck," she said loudly, and then in a whisper, "You'll need it."

Walter looked to see if Grandpa Walt had heard, but he was bent over, taking off his bowling shoes on a far bench. Walter turned away from Jennifer and faced the lane. "Zero in," he said to himself. "Don't let her get to you." He swung the ball back and forth, getting up his nerve. *I'll show her,* he thought, starting his approach to the lane.

Just as Walter was about to deliver the ball he heard Jennifer's voice. "Dribble, drabble, bad-luck start!"

Walter stumbled over his own foot and lurched over the foul line. This made a loud alarm buzz. A couple of kids laughed. Walter's face turned bright red as he quickly stepped back from the line. He wanted to hide.

Grandpa Walt was by his side in a flash. He slipped an arm around Walter's shoulder. "No big deal, Walt. Everyone steps over the line now and then. Right, Jen?"

"Right, Mr. Dodd," said Jennifer. "Tough luck, Walter."

Walter couldn't stand her innocent act another second. He pointed his finger at Jennifer. "It's all her fault! She jinxed me!"

Grandpa Walt's face clouded over.

"No excuses, Walter. We all have to take responsibility for our errors. It's been a long day. You're just tired. Now go and roll your last ball while I say good-bye to Mrs. Bumby." He gave Walter a pat on the back and walked off.

Walter felt like running after him to try to explain. Grandpa Walt had to understand. Besides, he didn't want to be left alone with Jennifer. He was *scared* to be alone with her. Walter glanced back to see if she was still there.

Jennifer was looking right at him. "Your grandfather told me about your baseball team. Were those kids you had lunch with today your friends from the Never Sink Nine?" She twirled a braid around a finger and smiled.

Snake braids, Walter thought. She had made him foul in front of the whole bowling center. "Yeah, they're my friends," he said angrily, "something you'll never have." It felt better being

66

angry with Jennifer than afraid of her, but not much better.

Jennifer looked hurt for a second. Then she stood and peered down at him, narrowing her eyes. She looked like a cobra ready to attack.

Walter took a step back and clutched his bowling ball.

Jennifer raised both hands and wiggled her fingers at him.

Double trouble, triple jinx,
All your balls will sink, sink, sink!

Walter's bowling ball slipped from his grip onto his foot. A sharp pain shot up his toes to his brain. "Ow-w-w-w!"

Jennifer watched him hop around on one foot. "If you're nice to me, I'll break the spell," she said.

"Go away! Just leave me alone, you jinx!"

"Don't say I didn't give you a

chance, Walter *Dud.*" Jennifer waited for his reaction, but Walter had hopped over to a farther lane. He wanted to take off his bowling shoes a safe distance away.

Grandpa Walt passed Jennifer as she was leaving. "Bye, Jennifer. See you at the tournament."

"Bye, Mr. Dodd," she said, flipping back her pointy braids. "Bye, Walter!"

Walter didn't answer. His face turned red as he struggled to loosen the knots on his shoelaces.

Grandpa Walt sat down beside him and lifted one of Walter's feet onto his lap. "Looks like Jennifer's got you all tied up in knots. Let me help you with those, sport." He expertly pulled the laces free.

"She jinxed me again," said Walter. "And it's starting to work."

"We're all a little nervous around girls, Walt. Even at my age." He picked up Walter's bowling shoes and took them over to the shoe rental counter to return.

Walter slipped into his sneakers and ran after him. "But this is different," he insisted. "She really jinxed me."

Grandpa Walt zipped up his jacket. "Jenny's just trying to get your attention. She's probably feeling a little lonely. Mrs. Bumby told me her parents are getting a divorce." He waved good-bye to Sid. "Time for us Pinheads to pack it in." He picked up his bowling bag and started out the door.

Walter grabbed his jacket and followed Grandpa Walt. No one was taking him seriously. How was he ever going to play in the Grand Tournament with a triple jinx? Walter could already see his balls going into the gutter just as Jennifer said they would.

Walter gulped and repeated her words. "Sink, sink, sink."

CHAPTER FIVE

Never Sink Nine Emergency

That night after dinner, Walter pulled the upstairs phone into the linen closet to make a private call. He knew only two phone numbers by heart, Grandpa Walt's and Mike Lasky's. He started dialing Grandpa Walt's number until he remembered Grandpa's date with Mrs. Bumby.

Walter sat in the dark, trying to imagine Grandpa Walt having dinner with his school librarian. Then he dialed the Laskys' house.

Mike answered. "Lasky residence, Mike speaking."

Walter always had to keep from laughing when he heard Mike answer the phone that way. He knew his mom made him do it. "Hi, it's me, Walter."

"Why're you whispering?"

"I'm in the closet."

"How come?" Mike whispered back.

"Jennifer triple jinxed me at the bowling alley today."

"So? You said it's just hocus-pocus."

"It's not. I'm throwing gutterballs. We've got to do something fast, or I'm going to bomb at the tournament."

"Don't panic," said Mike. "We'll call a Never Sink Nine emergency meeting tomorrow. How about the Pizza Palace?"

"Good idea," said Walter. Their team always ate there after every baseball game. Walter missed their weekly pizza visits when it wasn't baseball season. "I'll call Melissa, Pete, Otis, and Tony. You call Christy, Felix, and Katie."

71

Walter remembered all the times his Never Sink Nine friends had helped one another out before.

It was agreed. The nine of them would be sure to think up a solution to Jennifer's jinx.

The next day, the Never Sink Nine met at the Pizza Palace. They pooled their allowance money to buy a large pepperoni pizza with extra cheese and mushrooms and a round of sodas. By the time Walter finished explaining the Jennifer jinx, his slice of pizza was cold.

"Sounds like she hypnotized you." Pete wiggled his fingers, imitating Jennifer. He was an amateur magician.

Otis waited until he had finished his pizza. "I think you should tell Mrs. Bumby or your grandfather."

Walter shook his head. "They don't understand."

Melissa stood up and tapped her soda can to get everyone's attention. "From a medical point of view, I think you'll need an antidote."

Everyone looked at her with interest. Melissa was planning on becoming the first cowgirl doctor. She knew just what to do when someone got a cut.

Melissa continued. "Jennifer has given Walter gutterball syndrome, and he's going to need strong medicine to fight it."

Walter screwed up his face. "I'm not taking any medicine. I'll just have to drop out of the tournament."

"You can't quit and let Coach down," said Tony. "If you drop out, he can't play either."

Christy leaned forward. "There're nine of us and only one Jennifer. Maybe we should put a spell on *her*."

"But I don't know any." Walter was beginning to lose hope.

"It doesn't have to be an abracadabra spell," said Melissa. "How about a team spell, like a cheer? It works for other teams in trouble. We'll just make one up for the Pinheads."

No one looked convinced.

Walter checked his Babe Ruth wristwatch. It was two twenty-five. "I have to meet Grandpa Walt at Echo Bowl in five minutes." He slowly put on his jacket and Pinhead hat. He knew Jennifer and Mrs. Bumby would probably be there practicing, too.

"Cool hat," said Mike.

Walter tried to smile, but he couldn't.

Melissa whispered in Walter's ear. "Don't worry. Just work on bowling. We'll take care of the rest."

Walter zipped up his jacket and waved good-bye. "Thanks for trying." He wished he could believe what Melissa had said.

CHAPTER SIX

Pinhead Panic!

Every day after school that week Walter bowled with Grandpa Walt, and each day his scores got a little higher. But every time Jennifer walked by, Walter threw a gutterball.

Finally it was Saturday, the day of the tournament. Walter arrived at Echo Bowl loaded with good-luck charms. His pockets bulged with his lucky tooth, a rabbit's foot, and five marbles. Five was his lucky number. He also wore the lucky socks Grandpa Walt had given him after the Never Sink Nine's first baseball game. They had never been washed to keep in all the luck.

Lucky charms are my only chance, he thought, giving his socks a tug. He stopped to look at the table filled with trophies for the Grand Tournament winners. He imagined one next to Grandpa Walt's baseball trophy on his dresser. He could see Grandpa Walt emptying coins from his pocket into it.

Grandpa Walt walked up behind him and slipped an arm around his shoulder. "Hi, Walter. I was afraid you weren't going to show up. Checking out our trophy before we take it home?"

Walter sighed. He couldn't even look Grandpa Walt in the eyes.

Grandpa Walt put his hands on Walter's shoulders. "What's wrong, sport?"

Walter wanted to tell him how he

felt, but he couldn't. He twisted the long bowling pin–shaped hat in his hands and tried to explain. "We won't win any trophy. I'm not good enough."

Grandpa Walt shook his head. "That's not true. You're good enough to be my teammate, aren't you? Besides, I don't care about these silly trophies. All I want is to knock down a few pins today and have fun with my favorite grandson." He took the Pinhead hat and put it on Walter. Then he took an identical hat out of his pocket and pulled it down on his own head.

Walter's face lit up. "You got another hat."

"Of course. We're the Pinheads. We've got to have matching hats. We're a team." Grandpa Walt handed Walter his bowling bag to carry. "Let's go find our home lane," he said, leading the way.

Lane Five was marked "DODD." *A*

good sign, thought Walter, touching the five lucky marbles in his pocket.

Echo Bowl was packed, and the air was filled with excitement. Today the stars were kids and their grandparents. Walter felt like a celebrity walking around in his Pinhead hat. Since Grandpa Walt had one on, too, everyone knew they were teammates.

After Walter changed into his bowling shoes, he searched for his mom and dad in the crowd. They were sitting in chairs lined up behind the bowling alleys with the other parents. Tony Pappas was there, too, taking notes on all the teams for his newsletter.

"Coach is the highest scorer in the league, so you're the favorite to win," said Tony. "That is, if you don't get jinxed again. How did that jinx go? Dribble, drabble something?" He held up his pencil ready to write.

Walter's heart sank. For a few minutes he had almost managed to forget about Jennifer's jinx.

A voice came over the loudspeaker. "Echo Bowl welcomes you to the annual Grand Tournament for grandparents and grandchildren! Contestants, please find your lanes and begin your game. The two highest-scoring teams will be selected to play in the finals."

Through the crowd, Walter spotted two long snake braids. Jennifer! He ducked behind the soda machine before she turned around.

Melissa was putting her change into the soda machine when she saw Walter's Pinhead hat sticking out. "Walter? What are you doing back there?"

"I'm hiding from Jennifer," he whispered.

"Oh, that," she said, taking a gulp of soda. "Mike told me he figured out a way to break the jinx. He's coming as soon as he finishes helping his dad clean out their garage." Melissa hurried off to join her grandmother on Lane Ten.

"I'm triple jinxed and Mike's cleaning his dumb garage!" Walter gave the soda machine a little kick and an orange soda rolled out.

Sid walked over. He picked up the soda and handed it to Walter. "Looks like your lucky day, kiddo. Better get to your lane. The tournament's starting."

Some lucky day, thought Walter. He took a deep breath, checked to see that the coast was clear, and made a dash for Lane Five.

Grandpa Walt was ready to roll. His green and black ball was out of its bag and resting in the ball return. "You're the leadoff man, champ. I'll anchor." He handed Walter a bowling ball. "Don't forget the most important thing."

"What?" Walter tried to remember

Grandpa Walt's pointers. *Don't throw the ball. Bend your knee. Zero in.*

Grandpa Walt pulled Walter's hat over his eyes. "Have fun!"

Walter shoved his hat back up and grinned. He *had* forgotten that one.

"Walter!" His parents were waving at him.

Tony gave him a big thumbs-up sign.

Walter scanned the other lanes for Mrs. Bumby and Jennifer. They were six lanes away and Jennifer was busy bowling. *Maybe she's forgotten all about me*, he thought. *I'm safe.* He gripped the ball with his three fingers and stepped up to the lane.

Grandpa Walt was already cheering him on.

Walter took aim at the pins and approached the foul line. He swung the ball forward and let it go. It crept toward the pins. It was what veteran bowlers called a creeper or a powder-puff ball. Slow.

"Good ball control," said Grandpa Walt. "Slow and steady wins the race."

Walter slapped the side of his leg in frustration. He didn't care about slow and steady. He had wanted to start off the game with a powerhouse roll. Walter's eyes were glued on the ball as it barely reached the pins. It knocked down the headpin and pushed through, leaving only two pins standing in a wide-open split.

"Snake eyes!" yelled Grandpa Walt, scribbling down the score.

Walter heard clapping from behind him and turned around. Some of his friends from the Never Sink Nine had joined his family.

"Yeah, Pinheads!" roared Otis and Katie.

Felix was clapping so hard his glasses slid down his nose.

Walter felt as if he were a famous actor and the bowling alley were his stage. He scooped up his ball as it popped out of the ball return and took a bow.

"Encore!" said Grandpa Walt.

Walter didn't bother to take aim this time. He just stepped up to the foul line and threw the ball hard. It curved wide, teetering on the edge of the gutter. Walter held his breath and shoved his hand in his pocket to rub his lucky charms. At the last second the ball magically broke back into the center of the lane. It rolled right between the two standing pins into the pit.

Walter breathed a sigh of relief. No points, but no gutterball either. His lucky charms had worked!

"What a bender," said Grandpa Walt, getting up from behind the score table. He held a hand high in the air. "Give me five, partner."

Walter jumped up and slapped Grandpa Walt's hand in midair.

As Grandpa Walt picked up his bowling ball, the audience stopped talking to watch. No one cheered except Sid from the shoe rental counter.

"Hey, Kingpin! Sweep the deck!"

Walter knew Sid was telling Grandpa Walt to make a strike.

Grandpa Walt stood perfectly still, holding the ball up to his face to take aim. He quickly approached the lane, bent down on one knee, and extended his arm in one long, graceful movement. Before Walter could blink, the ball crashed into the pins, sending them flying in all directions. Walter thought he felt the power of the hit through the floorboards under his feet.

"What a splasher," said someone from the stands.

A few people clapped as Grandpa

Walt quietly took his seat and marked an *X* on the score sheet.

Walter stared at his grandfather as if he'd never seen him before. He had always heard Grandpa Walt was a powerful athlete as a young man, but he'd never seen him in action until recently. Grandpa Walt was always on the sidelines, coaching and cheering him on. Today it was Walter's turn to cheer.

"Yeah, Grandpa Walt! Go, King-pin!" Walter raised a fist in the air and gave Grandpa Walt a big smile.

Grandpa Walt grinned and gave Walter a little salute.

Half an hour later, the Pinheads had finished their ninth frame. Grandpa Walt had bowled all strikes and one spare. Walter had knocked down pins in every frame, and none had landed in the gutter. With only one frame left in the game, it looked as if the Pinheads would make it into the finals.

"Your turn, Walt." Grandpa Walt was already adding up their scores. "Our scores are looking good. I wouldn't be surprised if we made it to the finals."

"Great." Walter looked over at the trophy table and tried to imagine what one would look like on Grandpa Walt's dresser next to his baseball trophy. A voice ended his daydream.

"Aren't you done with your game yet? We finished ages ago." It was Jennifer.

Walter knelt down and pretended to tie his shoelace. Four marbles and his lucky tooth fell out of his pocket and rolled across the floor.

Jennifer burst out laughing and pointed to the tooth. "Are you carrying around your *baby* tooth?"

Walter's ears burned as he chased after his lucky charms and stuffed them back into his pocket. He stood up and faced her. "It's none of your business."

She looked at his bowling pin hat and snickered. "That's the funniest-looking hat I ever saw."

"It's supposed to be funny. That just shows how dumb you are."

Jennifer's eyes narrowed as she leaned forward and whispered,

Pinheads panic, fingers like butter,
All your balls land in the gutter.

She made wide bug eyes at him and wiggled her fingers in front of his face.

Walter backed away so fast he bumped into Grandpa Walt's chair at the score table.

"Shake a leg," said Grandpa Walt. "Let's finish up so there's time to grab a sandwich before the finals begin."

Walter tried to ignore Jennifer, but he couldn't. Every time he tried to pick up his bowling ball, it slipped through his fingers. His hands felt sweaty and his heart was racing. He was even afraid to touch his lucky charms in case they might fall onto the floor again. Finally he got his fingers in the holes and picked up the ball. He turned away from Jennifer and faced the lane. The same words kept running through his mind: *All your balls land in the gutter.*

"I'll show her," he muttered, stepping up to the line. Walter swung the ball around so hard his arm wrapped around his body, spinning him in a full circle. He ended up tangled in his own arms and legs.

Laughter rippled through the audience as Grandpa Walt came to his rescue. He untangled Walter. "Relax, Walt," he said, and gave his shoulder a squeeze.

Walter could feel Jennifer staring at him. He dropped the ball onto the

lane and watched it bounce into the gutter.

"First gutterball all day," Grandpa Walt said quickly. "You're doing great. Try again."

Walter tried not to panic as he waited by the ball return. He glanced at the crowd. His mother blew him a kiss and waved. Otis gave him another thumbs-up. But there was Jennifer, standing beside Mrs. Bumby, watching him.

Walter felt all his luck slip away as he threw the next ball without bending his knee. He helplessly watched it clunk down so hard it skipped over to the next lane and sank into its gutter.

Grandpa Walt leaped up and pointed to the ball. "Can't keep the Pinheads roped into one tiny lane!" Everyone laughed. "Good game, partner," he said, shaking Walter's hand. "I'll drop off our score sheet and meet you in The Grill. They'll announce the finalists during lunch."

The Never Sink Nine waited until Walter's family left for The Grill. Then they joined him on Lane Five.

"I saw her jinx you," said Tony. "Tough break."

"Me, too," said Katie. "Too bad Mike isn't here yet. I wonder what's holding him up."

Felix was squinting into the crowd. "Isn't that the jinx?" He pointed at a girl coming their way.

Walter wasn't waiting to find out. "I've got to go," he said, and made a beeline for the men's room.

Walter locked himself in a bathroom stall and sat down on a lowered toilet seat. "She's not jinxing me again. I'm never coming out of here."

CHAPTER SEVEN

Pinheads, Unite!

As he hid in the bathroom, Walter heard the finalists announced over the loudspeaker.

"Ladies and gentlemen, we are pleased to announce this year's Grand Tournament finalists: Mrs. June Bumby and her granddaughter, Jennifer Pittman, the Alleycats, will be playing against the Pinheads, Walter Dodd, Senior and Junior, on Lanes Seven and Eight in five minutes. See you there!"

Pete, Tony, Otis, and Felix burst into the bathroom to congratulate Walter.

"Walter! Where are you?"

"In here," Walter whispered. He knew they'd find him sooner or later.

"This is great! I'm going to do a cover story on you," said Tony.

"Come on out," said Otis. "You've only got five minutes. Coach is waiting."

"No."

"Come on, Walt," pleaded Pete. "Don't you want to take a crack at winning that giant trophy?"

"No. I'm not going to bomb in front of everyone. You know Jennifer's just going to jinx me again. You saw her do it." Walter waited for someone to argue with him. But no one said anything. They knew it was true.

Walter heard some whispering, and then he saw Tony's head poke up from under the stall door.

94

"You can't let Coach down," Tony said. "After all the times he's come through for us, it isn't fair. He's the one who made us a team in the first place. Besides, this is his trophy, too, you know."

Walter's heart sank. He knew Tony was right. Grandpa Walt had never let him down, and he couldn't let Grandpa Walt down now. He had to do it. Without another word, Walter stood up and unlocked the door. His friends swarmed around him and gave him a pat on the back.

"You're doing the right thing," said Felix.

Everyone nodded in agreement as Walter walked past and opened the bathroom door. Christy, Melissa, and Katie were waiting outside. When they saw Walter, they clapped.

Walter had one last hope. "Where's Mike?" he asked Melissa.

Melissa shrugged. "Sorry," she said, "He's still not here."

Walter bravely marched past his friends to Lane Seven.

"Where've you been?" asked Grandpa Walt. He was sitting next to Mrs. Bumby with one arm around her shoulder. "We missed you at The Grill. Hope you got something to eat. An athlete's got to keep up his strength."

"I'm okay." Walter forced a smile.

"We had a delicious lunch, didn't we, Jennifer?" said Mrs. Bumby cheerfully.

Jennifer looked straight at Walter. "I had a toasted peanut *butter* sandwich," she said, emphasizing the word *butter*.

Walter froze as he remembered her last jinx. *Pinheads panic, fingers like butter, all your balls land in the gutter.* "I'm a goner," he muttered.

"Did you say something, Walt?" asked his grandfather.

Walter shook his head. He had to be brave.

Everyone in Echo Bowl gathered around the two lanes. The crowd was so thick Walter couldn't see Sid back at the shoe rental counter. Danny waved at Walter. He had finished his paper route and joined their parents in the front row.

"Let 'er roll." Grandpa Walt handed Walter his bowling ball.

Walter looked over at Jennifer as she rolled a ball straight down the center of her lane. It knocked over several pins. Mrs. Bumby clapped and glanced over at Walter.

"Having fun, Walter?" she asked.

Walter nodded weakly. Even Mike couldn't save him now. Walter stood before the rows of bowling pins like a prisoner facing a firing squad and threw his first gutterball.

Three frames later, while Grandpa

Walt was piling up strikes, Walter was still throwing gutterballs.

Walter's spirits sank farther as he watched another ball drop into the gutter. His parents clapped politely. But even his Never Sink Nine friends had grown quiet. Walter looked down at his lucky socks sagging around his ankles. *Six more frames, and it'll all be over,* he thought.

"Walt!" Mike flung open the front door. It crashed back against the wall as he pushed his bike through. Everyone watched as Mike pedaled up the bowling alley to Lane Seven, balancing a big bag in his front bike basket. He leaped off his bike into the crowd, carrying the bag.

"I've got it!" he said, out of breath. He turned to Grandpa Walt. "We need a time-out, Coach."

Grandpa Walt looked amused, but he shook his head. "This isn't baseball,

Mike. There are no time-outs in bowling."

"Please," Mike pleaded. "It'll only take a second. I promise."

Grandpa Walt looked at Mrs. Bumby, who smiled and nodded her approval. Grandpa Walt talked to the tournament officials and returned with their answer.

"Okay, Mike. You've got exactly two minutes. No longer."

Before Grandpa Walt had finished his sentence, the Never Sink Nine had gathered around Mike in a team huddle. Walter crossed all his fingers, hoping for a miracle. When they finally straightened up, the Never Sink Nine were all wearing Pinhead hats! Mike led them into the front row as the crowd started laughing. "Okay, you can bowl now," he said to Grandpa Walt. But Grandpa Walt was doubled over laughing.

Walter couldn't help smiling. Every-

one's laughter had broken the tension. As he looked at his friends in their silly hats, the tournament didn't seem so serious anymore. He felt relaxed for the first time that day.

"First, a cheer!" said Melissa.

Mike pulled out a piece of paper and whispered the cheer to his friends.

The Never Sink Nine formed a line and hooked arms as they swayed left and then right, chanting, "Lean to the left, lean to the right, Come on, Pinheads, fight, fight, fight!"

They looked as if they were having such a good time several people in the audience joined them for the second chorus of "Pinheads, unite! Fight, fight, fight!"

Walter looked over at Jennifer. She had stuck her fingers in her ears to drown out their cheers. Suddenly she didn't seem so scary anymore. This time Walter didn't wait for Grandpa Walt to hand him a bowling ball. As he took aim at the pins, he glanced over at Jennifer again. She raised her hands and started to wiggle her fingers.

The Never Sink Nine stopped her short. "It's all right! Pinheads, fight!"

Jennifer dropped her hands and moved closer to her grandmother. Laughter and cheers filled the bowling alley.

The memory of Jennifer's jinxes faded away as Walter took aim on the pins. Grandpa Walt's words ran through Walter's head: *Relax, zero in, and carry through with the ball.*

Walter released the ball straight down the lane. It crashed into the pins as the Never Sink Nine stomped their feet and cheered. Walter punched the air and spun around.

Jennifer's jinx was broken!

Fifteen minutes later the game was almost over and Walter hadn't rolled one gutterball since the fourth frame. Mrs. Bumby and Jennifer had finished their game and their final score appeared on a board above their alley: 245. Walter was having so much fun he hadn't even thought about who was winning.

"This is our last frame, sport." Grandpa Walt was looking over their score sheet.

"What's our score?" asked Walter.

"Two thirty-six. We're running a strong second, unless we get real lucky."

"How lucky?" Walter looked over at Jennifer sitting on the sidelines. She looked sad, watching the Never Sink Nine joking around and having fun.

"We'd need a strike to win, but it doesn't matter. We've played a good game."

The Never Sink Nine began their cheer as Walter picked up his bowling ball. He wasn't thinking about Jennifer or the Never Sink Nine or even the trophy. He stared hard at the ten pins at the end of the lane and fired the ball. It rolled steadily along the wooden boards, slowing down as it reached the pins.

Walter's heart sank. The ball was moving too slowly to carry down all the pins. He held his breath as the pins began to topple, one by one. There was a moan from the audience as two wobbling pins were left standing. Walter began to turn away when one of the pins toppled over, knocking down the remaining pin. He had rolled a strike!

The Never Sink Nine threw their hats into the air as the crowd burst into cheers. Grandpa Walt rushed up to give Walter a big bear hug. Everyone swarmed onto the lane. Walter was kissed, hugged, slapped on the back, and his hand was shaken so many times he was dizzy.

After the excitement died down, Walter threw two bonus balls to complete the last frame. The Pinheads' final score appeared on a screen at the end of their lane next to the Alleycats' score. It was official. The Pinheads had won!

After the trophies were given out, the rest of the teams got ribbons. Melissa pinned her green ribbon onto her hair. Pete pinned his on his shirt. Everyone felt like a winner at the Grand Tournament party. Mike explained how he'd found the extra hats sorting through junk in the garage.

Tony took a photograph of Walter

and Grandpa Walt in their Pinhead hats holding the first-place trophy between them. Then he interviewed Walter for his newsletter. "Want to see my 'Sidelines' comic strip?" He showed them the cartoon he had sketched on the back of a score sheet. The Never Sink Nine looked like human bowling pins. Grandpa Walt was the kingpin.

Walter was passing around the cartoon when Jennifer walked up with a plate of big round brownies. "Want some bowling ball brownies? I made them myself last night."

For a second Walter was scared again. What if she wanted to poison him now that he had won the tournament? But everyone else took a brownie, so he did, too. Walter took a small bite. They were delicious. Chocolaty and gooey.

"Can I try on your hat?" she asked softly.

"Okay." Walter handed it to her.

Jennifer pulled it down over her bangs. "You look like a real Pinhead."

"Thanks." Jennifer smiled and bit into a brownie. She started to lift her other hand. Walter shrank back, waiting for her to wiggle her fingers. But she simply brushed some crumbs off her shirt. It looked as if Jennifer's jinxing days were over.

Later, after the party, Grandpa Walt drove the Never Sink Nine home in his station wagon just like the good old days after their baseball games. When everyone had been dropped off, Walter scooted across the front seat and leaned against Grandpa Walt. It had been a long day.

"That was nice of you to let Jennifer try on your Pinhead hat," said Grandpa Walt.

"She just felt left out."

Grandpa Walt nodded. He tapped the trophy cradled in Walter's lap.

"Where are you going to put that beauty?"

Walter lifted it and read the inscription:

ECHO BOWL
GRAND TOURNAMENT
FIRST PRIZE

Then he reached in Grandpa Walt's jacket pocket for a penny and dropped it inside. "It goes on your dresser next to the baseball trophy."

Grandpa Walt smiled. "Are you sure, Walter?"

"Yep." He looked up at his grandfather. "Can I be your teammate next year?"

"Count on it." Grandpa Walt honked his horn as they pulled into the Dodds' driveway. "Look out, Rockville! The Pinheads are coming back!"

ABOUT THE AUTHOR

GIBBS DAVIS was born in Milwaukee, Wisconsin, and graduated from the University of California at Berkeley. She has published several books for children, including *The Other Emily*. *Walter's Lucky Socks, Major-League Melissa, Slugger Mike, Pete the Magnificent, Tony's Double Play, Christy's Magic Glove, Olympic Otis, Katie Kicks Off,* and *Diamond Park Dinosaur* are all part of the Never Sink Nine series for First Skylark. Gibbs divides her time between New York City and Wisconsin.

ABOUT THE ILLUSTRATOR

GEORGE ULRICH was born in Morristown, New Jersey, and received his Bachelor of Fine Arts degree from Syracuse University. He has illustrated several

Skylark books, including *Make Four Million Dollars by Next Thursday!* by Stephen Manes and *The Amazing Adventure of Me, Myself, and I* by Jovial Bob Stine. He lives in Marblehead, Massachusetts, with his wife and two sons.

Patricia Reilly Giff and her Kids of the Polk Street School are back with three special books that teach you about counting and managing money, the post office and stamp collecting, and how to write your own book!

☐ 0-440-40929-2   COUNT YOUR MONEY WITH
                                 THE POLK STREET SCHOOL
                                 $3.99/$4.99 Can.

☐ 0-440-40973-X   THE POSTCARD PEST
                                 $3.99/$4.99 Can.

☐ 0-440-40882-2   WRITE UP A STORM WITH
                                 THE POLK STREET SCHOOL
                                 $3.50/$4.50 Can.

Bantam Doubleday Dell
Books for Young Readers

Bantam Doubleday Dell Books for Young Readers
2451 South Wolf Road
Des Plaines, IL 60018

Please send the items I have checked above. I'm enclosing $_____ (please add $2.50 to cover postage and handling). Send check or money order, no cash or C.O.D.s please.

Name _____

Address _____

City _____ State _____ Zip _____

Please allow four to six weeks for delivery.
Prices and availability subject to change without notice.   BFYR 33 7/94